Have
WAVELENGTH,
Will Travel

Have
WAVELENGTH,
Will Travel

Your travel guide to parallel universes.

Travels include:

Travel back to the beginning of time and
learn how The Almighty created
Heaven and Earth

Travel into the future and
check out your tomorrows

Travel next door – aliens are our
neighbors, not extraterrestrials

Dennett Berg Nelson

This book illustrates how wavelengths hold
the key to inter-universe travel.

iUniverse, Inc.
New York   Bloomington

Have WAVELENGTH, Will Travel

This is a work of fiction. All of the characters, names, incidents, organizations, and dialogue in this novel are either the products of the author's imagination or are used fictitiously.

iUniverse books may be ordered through booksellers or by contacting:

iUniverse
1663 Liberty Drive
Bloomington, IN 47403
www.iuniverse.com
1-800-Authors (1-800-288-4677)

ISBN: 978-1-4401-4488-2 (pbk)
ISBN: 978-1-4401-4489-9 (ebk)

Printed in the United States of America

iUniverse rev. date: 5/6/2009

To
Sharon, Bret and Petrea

Have WAVELENGTH, Will Travel

TABLE OF CONTENTS

PREFACE

Have WAVELENGTH, Will Travel fills the demand for proof that age-old beliefs are factual and can be proven beyond the shadow of doubt. The development of Quantum Mechanics/String Theory and other scientific principles enable scholars to now confirm that many other universes exist. Just to name a few, there is a time travel universe, there is a superior-being universe (home base for UFOs?) and there is even an infinite universe that is commonly referred to as Heaven. Of course, we have always known Heaven exists but explaining it and how we get there have always been elusive and difficult goals. Elusive and difficult up until now that is, as nowadays we have scientific explanations and principles that support our age-old beliefs. Here is how faith and science differ:

Faith – something we accept without proof.

Science – accepted principles, such as when in positive gravity and we drop a glass of water, we know it will hit the floor.

For instance, some of us have 'faith' that Methuselah lived for nearly a thousand years but the scientific principle of parallel universes now 'proves' such an extended life span is possible. The following chapters are full of proof that faith and science are molded in reality. On the other hand, science can rule out things that over the years some people have come to believe. Specifically many people 'believe' we have been visited by beings from outer space but that seems improbable given the distances involved. For instance, Pluto is only 4 Billion miles away but our nearest earthlike planet is 120,000,000,000,000,000 miles or one hundred twenty Trillion miles away. Let us assume we can travel at one million miles an hour (by the way, that is twenty-five times faster than our fastest rocket), then divide that speed into a hundred twenty Trillion miles – you do the math and you will find a roundtrip, two hundred forty Trillion mile voyage will take thousands of years (somewhere around 25,000 years). Wow, such distances, speed and time are mind-boggling which means if UFOs exist, and they may well exist, they probably come from an inner dimension, not from outer space. Examples of inner dimensions or parallel universes include various radio wavelengths. Our universe has room for radio waves but we cannot see them. Our universe with radio waves also has room for TV waves but we cannot see them. Our universe with radio waves and TV waves also has room for cell-phone waves but we cannot see them either. Each of these entities travels within their own tunnel so to speak so as not to interfere with each other. In a similar fashion, other universes tunnel right by us and it is our task to identify and connect with them. Understanding and managing wavelengths are the keys to travel into other dimensions.

INTRODUCTION

UFO supporters are partially right about our being visited by aliens; right in that we have aliens and unidentified flying objects but they do not come from outer space, they come from inner space. Inner space is a collection of several parallel universes that are all around us. A commonly known parallel universe is the fourth dimension otherwise know as time. You may not recognize the name Edgar Cayce but his achievements earned him Prophet status; unfortunately his travels to and from the fourth dimension happened before TV was available to sensationalize his achievements. And, at some point or points during your lifetime, you had that strange feeling that somehow what you are doing (for the seemingly first time) is actually a recreation of something you have done before. If so, you too have traveled to another dimension but did not know it. It was really your brainwaves linking with the wavelength of another universe; in this case it was the time universe that actually whisked you into the future albeit for just a brief moment or two. An advanced process of wavelength control explains UFOs and how an alien (Noah?) could visit Earth, and live for 950 years while the average life span of his earthbound counterparts might have been only 30 years or so (no penicillin in biblical times plus one in three women died during childbirth). Also religious skeptics have long used lack of proof as their basis to disbelieve in the Almighty and His promise of Eternal Life. Well, the long awaited proof of Eternal Life is here and can be explained using universally accepted scientific principles. Those principles include Quantum Mechanic/String Theory and those disciplines identify at least eleven dimensions, some of which are involve a combination of space and time. Those eleven dimensions are ubiquitous, i.e., they exist everywhere at the same time. They travel within individual tunnels, membranes or casings, which keep them separate from one another. Just like radio waves, they are all around us but we do not know they are there unless we have some kind of 'connection' to their existence.

This book will give us a common core of understanding and a perception of the very unique pathway that exists between universes and using that insight we will solve UFO mysteries, the Prophet mystery, the feeling of 'being there before' mystery and a few of the religious mysteries that have heretofore baffled historians. Wavelengths could be that common core of understanding, i.e., aim a radio wave toward a distant mountain – it bounces off and reflects back to its origin. Then reduce the frequency very methodically until no echo is received - if no echo is received it means the wave has dissipated or the wave has penetrated the membrane of a parallel universe and absorbed by its existence. The process of diluting wavelengths exists and it happens every day. It happens in our sleep (Chapter 3), and it happens every time there is a credible UFO sighting (Chapter 4) and it happens at the moment of death (Chapter 5). Each is explained in following chapters. The premise of this writing is to promulgate the notion that wavelengths are the key to inter-universe travel so settle in and learn exciting new concepts about other dimensions and how we get there.

CHAPTER 1
Wavelengths, Membranes
and Parallel Universes

Quantum Mechanics and String Theory (QMST) are branches of physics that explain the behavior of everything from particles smaller than atoms all the way up to the expanding cosmos. QMST also describe parallel universes and the possibility of time travel. Clearly paradox prevents us from changing what has already happened, i.e., we could not change any event that would preclude ourselves from being born; but we could learn how to pass through the membrane or casing that contains the time universe and view past or future moments as if looking through a two-way mirror. Like a jar full of marbles that leaves plenty of room for BBs, sand and water, our universe has plenty of room for other dimensions and it is our task to recognize their existence and learn how we move from one to another.

Parallel dimensions/universes are omni-present, i.e., they are present everywhere simultaneously. In order for them to occupy the apparent same space at the apparent same time and still retain their own distinction, some sort of membrane must enclose them; and access to those membranes must have a common denominator and that denominator is probably associated with waves/wavelength. Like radio waves that are ever-present, other universes are also ever-present and we just need the proper instrument to detect them, just as we need an instrument to detect and interpret radio waves. Like radio frequencies that can fill the airwaves without affecting each other, membranes and wavelengths of different universes can also fill space without affecting other dimensions. Once we learn to understand fluctuations in time and manage wavelengths, new beliefs will emerge and age-old beliefs will be confirmed. Remember, Edgar Cayce (Chapter 3) knew how to achieve inter-universe travel – after all, he made the trip several times and all we have to do is re-discover his technique and duplicate it. In addition to Edgar Cayce, superior beings have mastered wave control but we will discuss those beings in a later chapter as will we discuss our need to master wavelength control and master it prior to December 21, 2012 when the continued existence of Earth, as we know it, will become tenuous at best (Chapter 6).

Universes are separated by what we will call a membrane; some thin intangible barrier that keeps us apart. Each universe travels within its own membrane and has its own particular wavelength (wavelength, as we know, is the distance between two successive points in a wave), but identifying and connecting with other universes remain the challenge. To meet that challenge, the concept of travel between universes requires some basic understanding of wavelengths and how they can be used to facilitate moving into and out of the membranes that encompass other dimensions. Our first objective would be to identify the wavelength of a parallel universe, and then our second objective would be to manipulate our wavelength so that it corresponds with that of the other universe.

A fundamental property of energy is that it displays wavelike properties and wavelike properties can be observed. We can even 'see' some wave patterns and frequencies as they manifest themselves in an electroencephalogram (EEG) of our own consciousness and/or sub-consciousness.

To effect the transition into other dimensions, we must learn how to dilate our brainwaves until they correspond to that of another dimension, whether it be the time dimension or another parallel universe, maybe the one that we have long known to be Heaven. Glucose driven metabolism keeps our mind and brainwaves confined to a particular point in time and space. Once our mind is released from that restraint it can seek out, match up and cycle right into another universe. In a very popular science fiction series, the beamer picked us apart particle by particle, and then reassembled all the particles at another location. Beamers are great but they are machine dependent, i.e., what would happen if it broke while you were disassembled – would your liver end up in one country and your feet in another? Wavelengths, on the other hand, only require a corresponding match to succeed. Wavelength management will soon become a new discipline and once we are able to manage glucose driven metabolism and change wavelengths, we will flow from medium to medium as long as the wavelengths are compatible. The universality of wavelengths (distance, oscillation etc) makes it possible to go wherever whenever, just find and understand the technique that allows us to match our wavelength with the wavelength of the where and the when, then we simply move into that medium. Membranes separate dimensions and each dimension is a universe of its own. Passing through the membrane is the challenge and using the process of elimination, we will find a solution that will allow us to penetrate such a barrier. Using wavelengths as the starting point, we will focus on the electromagnetic spectrum, the long and weak waves on one end and the short and strong on the other end. Since universes are identified by certain wavelengths, let us establish Earth as having a 'standard' wavelength measured in terms of visible light (somewhat of an average sized wavelength but not dangerous). In observing extremes, it is unlikely that other universes would take on any of the dangerous attributes associated with x-rays/gamma rays so the wavelengths governing parallel universes are probably somewhere between radio waves and infinite waves. Radio waves are categorized as being able to change direction, i.e., they bounce off submarines, airplanes, mountains, and our atmosphere just to mention a few, and any waves longer than those could be likely candidates to support a universe of their own. Now let us look for something between radio waves and the very long wavelengths. Edgar Cayce's experiences while in a state of deep sleep give us clues of where to look for those other universes and this book will pursue those clues. To illustrate the length and size/strength of wavelengths, here is how they compare to known entities:

TYPE OF WAVE	SIZE/STRENGTH
Infinite wave	Infinite waves are endless and able to traverse the selective barriers (membranes) that separate universes/dimensions. Infinite waves are associated with Eternal Life (Chapter 5).

Intermediate wave	This wave is several miles long and could extend to the infinite. It too can traverse the selective barriers (membranes) that separate universes. Intermediate waves are associated with the 4th Dimension (Chapters 2 and 3) and UFOs (Chapter 4).
Radio waves	A radio wave is from the width of a BB to several miles in length. It can enter membranes (sonograms) or bounce off buildings.
Microwaves	Microwaves are about the size of a tittle (the dot over an 'i'). They can heat up meals.
Infrared waves	These waves are the size of a one-celled creature and can warm the skin at the beach.

Visible light waves	Light waves are the width of bacteria and can activate the human eye. We will designate these waves as standard waves.
Ultra-violet waves	UV waves are the width of a virus and can cause sunburn.
X-ray waves	X-rays are about the size of an atom and can pass through flesh.
Gamma ray waves	Gamma rays are the size of an atom's nucleus and are the strongest of all waves. They can pass through metal.

It is easy to observe that the short, strong wavelengths within the electromagnetic spectrum are very dangerous and in fact hazardous to existence. We can therefore conclude that membranes that separate universes have a defensive mechanism against high energy, maybe a mirror to deflect high energy or, like negative gravity, some type influence that repels the damaging waves. Since it is therefore unlikely that short, damaging wavelengths do not hold the key to entering another membrane/dimension, let us focus on radio waves that are located at the longer end of the spectrum and compare them to brainwaves, which vary individually yet collectively fall within radio wave range. Here is how we interpret brainwaves as they are displayed on an EEG – notice the potential to match them with other realities.

BRAINWAVES/ACTIVITY

Longest brainwaves – eternal
Long brainwaves – deep sleep
Shorter brainwaves – alert and active

Once we learn to dilate and control brainwaves (like Edgar Cayce did), travel to other dimensions will become a matter of routine. Let us start with manipulating our brainwaves and do some serious time travel.

CHAPTER 2
The Time Universe – The 4th Dimension

The fourth dimension (the time universe) cannot be seen or felt but it is just as real as the other dimensions. As mentioned before, science has identified at least eleven other dimensions, four of which are space-time dimensions. One of those four is a time dimension in and of itself, and a universe of its own. Like a tubular membrane that has paralleled our universe for eons, the time dimension sleeve extends endlessly into our past while at the same time gradually collects our tomorrows as it expands forward. Just because we do not understand something does not mean it mean it does not exist. Entering the time universe is just like entering any other universe, we just dilate our brainwaves until they match the wavelength of the other universe, traverse the membrane and then sort of 'pulsate' into that dimension.

Once we enter the fourth dimension, the vortex of time sends us in the direction that corresponds to strength of our brainwaves. Remember our EEG and how a graph illustrated our brainwaves from the long and weak (deep sleep) to the short and strong (alert and active)? Stronger brainwaves mean more resistance at the vortex and we are moved forward in time; the weaker our brainwaves, the less opposition and the vortex whisk us into history. We will discuss our tomorrows later but right now, let us concentrate on those long and weak brainwaves that will carry us into the past. Through wave control (the same wave control that was used by Edgar Cayce to travel into the future) or an instrument of brainwave control, all we do is manipulate/dilate our brainwaves till they match the wavelength of the time dimension and, like a key unlocking the front door, we will zip into the fourth dimension and enter the vortex of time. Since we are on a long and weak brainwave, the vortex scoots us into the past. A quick trip back into time confirms realities that were only speculations before this writing. Imagine the crimes that could be solved once we master the speed of which our trips take us. But for now, let us take a quick first hand tour of Earth's history and beyond.

To expedite the trip, let us continue to dilate our brainwaves and zip back to the beginnings of time; then shorten the waves in spurts until we pop back to the present: Here is a chance to describe the beginnings of our expanding universe. Astrophysicists and cosmologists coined the term 'Singularity', and then went about defining the term as to how it applied to the Big Bang. But their problem has always been 'Where did the single entity come from'? We now know the Big Bang did not start with an undefined 'Singularity', it started with something more easily understandable and I call it 'Double-larity' – that is where two opposite quantities, each described by QMST as having their own existence, collide and the products of their collision annihilate one another and produce massive energy. Those quantities are 'nothing' and 'anti-nothing', and the chain reaction created by their collision resulted in enormous energy otherwise known as the Big Bang. Doublelarity is therefore the only explanation that proves the Big Bang started with absolutely nothing, zero, zip, and zilch. Here is how it happened. Hitching a ride on the time travel express we zoom back to before the Big Bang where we find infinite nothingness and the historical boundary of time itself. It is here where we find that the Almighty, another of the eleven universes, twitches and nudges the previously mentioned anti-nothingness and it is that twitch and nudge that sends anti-nothingness on a collision course with its opposite force. As anti-nothingness crisscrossed nothingness, the words collision and friction were coined. The collision of opposites, like metal meeting a grinder, spewed friction created entities (photons) and anti-entities (anti-protons) into an area that became know as space. When entities collide with anti-entities, they annihilate one another and release vast amounts of energy. That energy reformed photons into protons, the building block of a hydrogen atom, and hydrogen, as we know, is the most abundant element in the Universe. And when greater energy (a rapid succession or perhaps a combination of annihilations) was applied to protons, they converted into neutrons and other nuclear components that make up the remainder of the elements. Since nothingness and anti-nothingness are endless, the creation process continues indefinitely and that steady source of energy is what drives our expanding universe. Here is an 'equivalence expression' that substitutes an equal for an equal – it may better describe how Doublelarity (nothingness/anti-nothingness) created the universe

> Nothingness colliding with anti-nothingness generated friction created photons (light) and anti-photons (anti-light). From nothingness/anti-nothingness (doublelarity) we now have light/anti-light and the second step in the chain reaction that led to the Big Bang.

> Accumulated light colliding with anti-light created annihilation and the most powerful explosion ever known (The Big Bang). The original collision (doublelarity) resulted in photons and anti-photons. The annihilation of photons and anti-photons created the Big Bang – doublelarity now equals the Big Bang.

The enormous energy of the Big Bang created protons. The collision resulted in photons (light) and anti-photons (anti-light). The annihilation of photons and anti-photons created the Big Bang. The Big Bang created protons – doublelarity now equals protons.

The strong atomic force in nature pulls two protons together and they become hydrogen (one proton remains a proton and the other converts into an electron). The original collision resulted in photons (light) and anti-photons (anti-light). The annihilation of photons and anti-photons created the Big Bang. The Big Bang created protons and three protons became hydrogen – doublelarity now equals hydrogen.

Hydrogen is the most abundant element in the Universe and the building block for all other elements. In our equivalence expression, we can now substitute the universe for hydrogen – doublelarity and the chain reaction it produced now equals the Universe/Cosmos, as we know it.

Eureka, our trip back into time has already solved the age-old mystery of how our universe began and I challenge our cosmologists to prove it wrong.

Let us speed up our wave and move forward by leaps and bounds. We find the Earth forming billions of years ago.

And, as we wander back toward the present, we notice the earth was occasionally bombarded with gamma rays from distant super novas. As we know from previous chapters, gamma rays are the strongest and deadliest of all known sources of energy and their reoccurring visits to Earth was the catalyst for our evolution. Here was how gamma bursts from outer space affected life on earth. The ozone layer is the part of our atmosphere that absorbs large doses of the sun's ultra-violet (UV) radiation. UV is dangerous and particularly dangerous to RNA, those little message networks that connect DNA and any damage, even minor damage, to those complex systems could alter our blueprint for development. Growth and normal development was 'business as usual' until a burst of gamma rays entered our solar system and blew away our protective layers of defense. Gamma bursts are random, normally associated with exploding stars, maybe super novas, and last only a few seconds. But in those few seconds, the gamma burst was so strong it blew away part of our ozone layer and exposed life forms (and RNA/DNA) to prolonged UV radiation. The ozone layer eventually returned to normal but not before the gamma rays/UV rays changed the blueprints for development. Here is the evolution of earth/species in a nutshell.

4-5 bya (billion years ago) – after a violent beginning, Mother Earth gradually became productive and single celled micro-organisms began to thrive.

2.5 bya – multi-celled creatures emerged and it is here where intense UV radiation began its 'alterations'.

900 mya (million years ago) – after a series of UV induced 'modifications', marine invertebrates began to develop.

750 mya – a strong gamma ray burst caused devastating damage to the earth and its

atmosphere/ozone layer. Without their full insulating effect, radiational cooling led to a global ice age.

600 mya – after more gamma bursts and increased UV radiation, some invertebrates mutated into vertebrates and some of those became what we know as fish – the first creatures characterized as having a segmented backbone or spinal column.

430-600 mya – several more UV ray attacks further altered prehistoric DNA and air breathers (an elementary form of today's mudskippers) emerged from the sea. This is another major step in development and is the culmination of several minor yet progressive changes brought about by gamma ray bursts affecting numerous solar systems in Orion's Arm.

305-430 mya – once air breathers had developed, moderate changes in RNA/DNA appeared and after several gamma ray/ UV ray bombardments, our air breathers gradually developed into reptiles.

185-305 mya – progressive alternations turned some reptiles into dinosaurs and they flourished for millions and millions of years.

185 mya – another major development took place when radiated RNA of some species caused their DNA to create feathers instead of scales. We now call those creatures birds. Remember the age-old question – which came first, the chicken or the egg? The answer is – the chicken's egg came first as its layer (mother) was actually a different creature whose egg DNA had been changed by UV radiation; therefore its eggs hatched with feathers instead of scales. So from mutation, initial 'bird' eggs were the first of their species and later developed into all kinds of feathered creatures, including chickens.

65-185 mya – an absence of gamma bursts allowed dinosaurs to dominate the animal world, a domination that lasted for millions and millions of years.

65 mya – oops, after the long absence of exploding stars, one very powerful gamma

ray burst occurred about 65 million years ago and brought about the extinction of the dinosaurs. The burst was either enormous in size or too close to Earth and bombarded our prehistoric creatures with a lethal dose of both gamma and UV radiation. The extinction was relatively instant as this episode affected the DNA that controlled life support functions rather than just causing minor changes in appearance and/or features. Dino DNA could not withstand the most powerful rays in the electromagnetic spectrum so the dinosaurs made their entry into oblivion. However small mammals living underground survived and, even though radiation levels changed their DNA, the dose for them was not fatal. Extinction gamma/UV radiation also explains why no fossils are found in the K-T boundary, the K-T being the fallout period from an asteroid collision during which, one theory has it, all dinosaurs were destroyed. If the K-T killed the dinosaurs, then the boundary should include both K-T fallout and fossils of those dinosaurs it killed. However, the K-T boundary does not include fossils because the gamma/UV rays arrived first and had already laid the dinosaurs to rest.

32 mya – this particular gamma ray burst rearranged the flow of information within some mammals and we gradually metamorphosed into primates.

>200,000 years ago – the most recent gamma burst once again blew away part of the ozone layer and allowed the sun's UV rays to inflict damage to our primate ancestors. In the same fashion as they did 2.5 billion years earlier, UV rays destroyed the weakest RNA. Messages to DNA were subsequently rerouted and some primates developed into many manlike creatures. Some like Cro-magnum and Hobbit did not survive whereas, over hundreds of generations, Homo Sapiens took hold and, through natural selection, they began to thrive. It is interesting to note that the last gamma/UV event resulted in an RNA/DNA change that affected skin color. The electromagnetic force that encircles the Earth influences cosmic radiation and there is greater radiation at the poles than at the equator. Those varying degrees of radiation

resulted in the diversity of skin color; i.e., the DNA of man nearest equatorial Earth developed one color, whereas the DNA for man in temperate regions developed another color and those closer to the poles developed a color of their own as well as some different facial characteristics. Natural selection took its course and, wouldn't you know, here we are.

>100,000 years ago – the long-standing question of how the Aborigines settled Australia is finally answered. The answer also explains the missing stepping stones between Asia and North America, as well as the disappearance of Atlantis. All were located along tectonic plates and natural forces, such as volcanoes and earth slides (like the one pending in Las Palmas, Canary Islands), eliminated the land formations previously used as stepping stones for trans-continental travel and those forces also caused the total destruction of the ancient civilization known as Atlantis.

Continuing forward in time, many other mysteries are solved. For instance, the events leading to several catastrophic accidents

(Challenger, Flt 800, Flt 111, Flt 990 and Columbia) are particularly astonishing. The sequence leading to those disasters began in 1908 when a crystal-carrying comet exploded over Tunguska, Siberia. The crystals next appeared in a research lab near the Black Sea where they became the main components for a laser initially used to measure speed and distance. A practical test for the laser was to document the telemetry of the Shuttle Challenger, however a power surge amplified its strength and instead of measuring speed and distance, it blew a hole in the booster and the shuttle exploded. Glasnost and the fall of the Soviet Union allowed unscrupulous scientists to sell the laser to the highest bidder, which, at the time, were Middle-East extremists. Those extremists, in turn, used the laser to rein fear on their enemies. Flight 800 was blown from the sky to eliminate a passenger who happened to be the man who brokered the laser sale between the scientists and the extremists. The two scientists who sold the laser were eliminated when the flight they were on, Flight 111, was blown from the sky by their own creation. The destruction of Flight 990 eliminated one of their traitors and then, in the most spectacular display of accuracy and power, the Shuttle Columbia was mortally wounded while it was still in orbit, presumably to assassinate a popular enemy politician. Fortunately the laser was located and destroyed before its sights were set on Air Force One.

And along our travels, the infamous murder in Brentwood California will be solved, much to the surprise of many. Time travel may make you the greatest sleuth of all time.

CHAPTER 3
Interpret the Present and Enter Tomorrow

As mentioned in the previous chapter, the sleeve of time extends into ancient history while at the same time bulges forward into our tomorrows. On the way to our tomorrows, let us pause and take a closer look at the present and explain what people have long known as apparitions or ghosts. Apparitions and ghosts are really time travelers who, during their journey through time, sometimes pass weak spots in the membranes that separate our universe and the universe from where they originate. The weak spot allows the traveler to partially materialize and that is what gives it the 'ghostly' effect. It should be noted that the location of these weak spots/thinner areas do not change – they remain in the same places on the membranes as both universes travel through space. That means, in our universe, if the thin area is located in a castle's upstairs bedroom, that area is always where a partially materialized time traveler will appear. Or that constant weak spot may be in the wine cellar of an old mansion, or in a dungeon, or in the cargo hold of a ship. Wherever time travelers appear, the location signifies a thin membrane and becomes a prime spot for repeated sightings. Ever ask why ghosts only manifest themselves at night? That is because membranes are sensitive to high-energy waves and as a defensive mechanism; they repel those high-energy waves (x-rays, UV rays, Gamma Rays) and, at the same time, the repel process also strengthens/reinforces the two membranes. Time travelers are normally discreet however sometimes an unscrupulous traveler may decide to raise havoc by portraying a ghoul or some similar scary character in which case you will want to 'purge' it from the room. It is actually easy to rid ourselves of an unwanted visitor, just give it an overdose of high-energy waves, i.e., a portable x-ray machine would be best. Aim the x-ray at the point where the ghost was last seen, give it a burst and the weak spot/thin area of the membranes will go into its defensive posture, and part of that process includes rejuvenating and strengthening itself. Walla, the weak spot/thin area regenerated itself and the time traveler can no longer partially materialize at the point where the two universes previously touched.

We have traveled back to the beginning of time; we have stopped those pesky time travelers from annoying us, now it is time for the vortex to send us into that part of the time universe that bulges forward. And it is travel into our tomorrows that brings us the best evidence that the time universe really exists and to Edgar Cayce who pioneered travel into the 4th Dimension. You may not know of Edgar Cayce but he was dubbed 'The Sleeping Prophet' because, while in a state of deep sleep, he would assimilate knowledge from the future and upon awakening, he would relay the same to his inquisitive client. Could it be that while in that state of deep sleep, Edgar Cayce was able to dilate his brainwaves, match them up with the fourth dimension and ride into the future? It certainly seems more than a coincidence that the Sleeping Prophet acquired his foreknowledge when his brainwaves were dilated to an extreme (remember the EEG where the longer brainwaves signified deep sleep?). Later on, your 'personal' experience will add credibility to the premise that sleeping brainwaves can connect with the time universe but right now let us concentrate on Edgar Cayce's accomplishments in the early 1900s. The first few times Cayce visited the future were probably unintentional but once he realized such travel was possible he learned to duplicate the 'dilate' process and visited his tomorrow's on a frequent basis. In fact, he became so proficient; he could even accomplish the feat 'by appointment'. Yes, Cayce knew the secret of matching wavelengths and it is the challenge of our bio-physiological researchers to re-discover his technique so we too can become time travelers. The human body is mildly magnetic which is good news for our researchers because if the body is magnetic, it means it has a wavelength and with wavelength identification and management, we too can pulsate our way into other dimensions.

Edgar Cayce made 'intentional' trips into the future, however, on a few occasions, everyday people like you and me make unintentional trips into the future. Yes, most of us have made the trip but we did not know it, or at least at the time we did not know it. To put your unintentional trip differently, at one time or another you, or someone you know, entered a room for seemingly the first time, then had that eerie feeling that you had been there before, as if in a precognitive dream. Well, here is the real explanation of a precognitive dream and exactly how you had experienced the event before. During a deep sleep, your dilated brainwaves matched the wavelengths of the time dimension and you skipped into the future and viewed the event in your tomorrows. Then later on, time caught up with what was previously the future and you experienced the event just as you saw it in the earlier trip into your tomorrows. Yes, time travel is possible – Edgar Cayce did it with regularity and you actually experienced the process when your deep sleep brainwaves matched up with the 4th Dimension and your tomorrows.

CHAPTER 4
The Advanced Universe

We have been through our universe (the Standard Universe), the fourth dimension (the Time Universe), now it is time to delve into to the Advanced Universe which holds the key to solving numerous mysteries including UFOs, famous people from the Bible, and that advanced civilization from early Earth history known as Atlantis. The advanced universe is similar to the time universe in that it lies within its own casing and has a periphery not unlike the time membrane. It expands and contracts and its inhabitants (we will call them the Advancelots) travel to and from other universes as easily as we move from one room to another. On the intelligence scale, they are about as far above us as we are above Neanderthal. Everything that produces energy has a wavelength and that includes our own bodies. At our 'meager' level of intelligence and achievement, we are unable to consciously manipulate our 'personal' wavelengths and zip into another universe but not so with the Advancelots, for they have conquered wavelength control and have the expertise to pop in and out of other universes as if access were through a revolving door. Some of their past voyages have triggered our imagination and we will recount just a few of them, starting with UFOs which are actually vehicles from a parallel universe, not from outer space.

The reason UFOs come from parallel universes is obvious once we realize the vast distances aliens would have to travel to get from whatever distant point they originate all the way to earth. Let us refer to some Astronomy 101.

Solar system – our sun with its eight planets is a solar system. A group of solar systems with a common nucleus is called a galaxy.

Nearest Solar system with planets – Alpha Centauri is the closest star to our own that has planets (8 by the way). By astronomical standards, Alpha Centauri is not very far away – a mere 24 trillion miles, that is 24 followed by twelve zeros.

Milky Way – our galaxy, the Milky Way, contains 100 billion solar systems and is one quintillion miles wide, that is a one followed by eighteen zeros (1,000,000,000,000,000,000) or a billion billions.

Andromeda - The Great Nebula (Andromeda) is the nearest galaxy to the Milky Way and is 20 quintillion miles away, that is twenty followed by eighteen zeros (20,000,000,000,000,000,000) or twenty billion billions. That's a long way from home, Toto.

Speed – if we could travel at the speed of light (671 million miles an hour), it would take 100,000 years to go from one end of the Milky Way to the other.

Get the picture; even at the speed of light the distances are just too great for aliens to travel and 'arrive alive'. Many of us believe in extraterrestrials and UFOs but now since it is obvious they do not come from outer space, we must look for another place for them to originate. That other place of origin is probably the parallel universe we call the Advanced Universe and those extraterrestrials are actually 'inner'-terrestrials who we will call 'Advancelots'. The Advancelots have mastered wavelength control over their mind, their body and other material things, as well as the membranes that separate our respective universes. And by mastering the wavelength of their body, they can physically enter other universes and return home just by redirecting their wavelengths. Using wave control they can easily open membranes and move their transportation devices (unidentified flying objects) from one dimension to another. That explains why UFOs seemingly pop in from nowhere and then disappear just as rapidly. Their ability to control wavelengths also explains why UFOs are not identified on radar, the same powerful radar that is capable of monitoring small pieces of space debris/space junk that orbit the earth.

UFO wavelengths are so dilated that what appears to their making a high speed, right angle turn in our time, is actually an elongated, sweeping turn in their time. This time-differential also reveals itself later when we discuss Methuselah but right now let us continue to focus on UFOs. Since wavelength management is the key to Advancelot travel, there is no reason why such management does not extend to absorbing waves produced by sound – that would explain why UFOs are silent and why their terrific speeds do not result in sonic booms. Descriptions of UFOs vary from sighting to sighting but remember the aerodynamic restrictions of our universe do not necessarily apply to other wavelengths. The combination of no sound, no shape restrictions and rapid acceleration suggest some kind of levitation and/or anti-gravitational propulsion. In any event, it is more likely that aliens and UFOs are from inner-space and not from distant planets where travel time, even at the speed of light, would exceed tens of thousands of years.

Aliens have been visiting for thousands of years but we did not recognize them as aliens because Advancelots, like all mankind, are made in the image of God. Oh oh, another religious reference (remember it was the Almighty who originally nudged nothing and anti-nothing so they would collide and create the Big Bang). Yes, **Have WAVELENGTH, Will Travel** bears out many biblical events and best of all, science and wavelength control now explain how all those age-old beliefs actually happened. Let us skip back to Noah's grandfather, Methuselah, whom was the champion of long-life. He lived for 969 years but how could that happen you ask when life expectancy at that time was probably 30 to 35 years? Let us introduce the Advancelots again and their ability to manage their body's wavelengths and create time differentials between the functions commensurate with their universe and the functions commensurate with ours. As a probable visitor from the advanced universe, Methuselah was functioning at a rate corresponding to his universe whereas his earthbound counterparts were functioning at a much faster rate, a faster rate associated with the natural forces that govern life on earth. Moving forward toward the present, another long-life graced our history and the famous Ark was named for him. Could it be that Noah had the same inner-terrestrial bodily functions as his grandfather because he too lived for more than 900 years?

Advancelots not only graced our history with people of long-life, they also had travelers of great wisdom, reason and knowledge. One particular traveler entered an ancient society of pagans and idol worshipers. His compassion and understanding, and His words of wisdom, insight and perception immediately elevated Him to prophet status. As someone who had just stepped through a membrane into our world, His presence was unexplainable so He gave the people something known as 'faith' and applied the term to things they could not comprehend. For instance, it was easier to have 'faith' in Heaven than to explain the existence of a parallel universe to someone living in an era where one's two feet were the most common form of transportation. Yes a deity (The Almighty) caused the Advancelots to visit Earth and it was therefore easier to say a deity was responsible for unbelievable events than quote a science the locals could not understand. And having 'faith' that He 'ascended into Heaven' better explained His disappearance than trying to prove He changed wavelengths and hitched a ride back to the Advanced Universe or changed wavelengths to enter the Eternal Universe (next chapter). Other travelers of great wisdom could have used names such as Abraham, Moses, Buddha, Confucius or maybe even Mohammad to name just a few.

Speaking of wisdom, reason and knowledge, maybe the Advancelots established a colony here on Earth. You guessed it, they did and that colony was called Atlantis; and as we know, it was inhabited by a peaceful, intellectual and architecturally advanced race of people. Of course the Advancelots ended their vacation and went back through their membrane prior to the geological disaster that blew Atlantis from the face of the earth. However subsequent Advancelot visitors traveled to several places in the known world and taught the basics wherever they went. If the locals were interested in pottery, they taught advanced pottery, if interested in ship building, they taught naval architecture and gave them the knowledge of using sails, and then what about the pyramids? Acting alone, the Egyptians could not have been wandering the desert one day and building the Sphinx and great pyramids the next. They needed architectural knowledge and that knowledge came from a traveling educator from the Advanced Universe. With the traveler as their mentor, the Egyptians gained a basic knowledge of engineering and through clever use of existing resources; they constructed monuments that lasted for thousands of years. And, what about the Mayan Empire? The Mayans were not just picking cocoa beans one day then erecting pyramids and creating sophisticated calendars the next. Strange, or is it a coincidence, that their calendar ends on December 21, 2012 (see Chapter 6). Maybe their mentor was an Advancelot too. Stonehenge is a very sophisticated megalith. Were pre-Druids tending sheep one day and the next day capable of mathematically identifying both the longest day of the year and the shortest day of the year? And what about those colossal etchings in Peru – without help, how could potato farmers have been planting spuds one day and the next day drawing huge complex figures that could only be viewed from the sky? It appears the Advancelots were teaching at all over the world.

CHAPTER 5
The Eternal Universe

We have discussed Earth as being the 'standard' universe (Universe number 1), the Time Universe (Universe number 2), the Advanced Universe (Universe number 3) and now it is time to discuss the Eternal Universe (Universe number 4). Yes, an old belief that is about to be confirmed is the parallel universe called Heaven. Like the standard universe, the time universe and the advanced universe, Heaven has a membrane of its own and passage through the membrane requires a wavelength match unique to Eternity. So far, passage through the Eternal membrane has been a one-way trip although some people claim to have been there as visitors only. Remember the EEG and how the wavelengths of our 'essence' were reflected on the graph? And do you remember the 'infinite wave' where the wavelength is endless and able to traverse selective membranes that separate universes/dimensions? Now, how does the wavelength of our 'essence' merge with the infinite wavelength of Eternity? The answer is, we must dilate our 'essence' and keep dilating it until it matches the wavelength of Heaven itself. That happens at the moment of death when our glucose driven metabolism can no longer generate the energy needed to keep our essence confined to a particular point in time and space. Our wavelengths then dilate until their frequency corresponds to the parallel universe called Eternity and we slip right into Heaven. Oh yes, QMST has room for yet another universe and that universe could very well be called Hades. Let us speculate, maybe a wavelength burdened with guilt would bypass Eternity and plummet right into that other space time continuum fearfully known as Hades. We have always had faith that Heaven existed and now, through a new understanding of wavelengths, we have science confirming that Eternal Life actually exists.

Let us recap how science explains and confirms some age-old beliefs.

God created Heaven and Earth – According to science and doublelarity, it was The Almighty who caused two entities to collide and create the friction and spark needed to unleash the Big Bang. Of course Heaven is a dimension with an infinite wavelength, therefore, to The Almighty, the term 'In the beginning', amounted to a matter of days while the equivalent time in the standard universe equaled billions of years.

Methuselah lived for almost a thousand years – the existence of a parallel universe called the Advanced Universe explains how people with different metabolisms could visit Earth and remain here for an extended time.

Noah lived for 950 years – he too could have been an Advancelot whose metabolism allowed him an extended stay on Earth, make an Ark and survive the flood.

Our Teacher ascended into Heaven – He too could have been from another dimension and His unique metabolism allowed Him to survive torture then disappear into a parallel universe.

The existence of Heaven – the existence of parallel universes allows for a variety of dimensions, one of which has wavelengths consistent with infinity. Brainwaves at the moment of death appear to stop but in fact they dilate and continue to dilate until they match up with the infinite waves associated with Eternal Life.

Other famous religious leaders – Abraham, Moses, Buddha, Confucius, and maybe Mohammed too, could very well have been visitors from a parallel universe. After all, their wisdom, philosophy, phraseology and concise verbiage are atypical or uncharacteristic of the rudimentary civilizations associated with their eras, therefore each must have been nurtured elsewhere, a parallel universe maybe. For example, because people in that time frame could only understand basic terminology, ancient texts depict The Teacher frequently being assisted by a young boy because the juvenile's limited communication skills allowed the masses to better grasp the message.

Maybe you do not like the term 'Advancelot' to describe the people from the Advanced Universe so let us change their name to something more familiar and that name could be 'Angel'. Like we used substitution to help express Doublelarity, let us substitute Angel for the word Advancelot. Their 'Halo' could actually represent a device to control wavelengths and therefore scientifically explain their moving from one dimension to another. Right from the start, we have been saying The Almighty was 'causing' things to happen so let us look at some events from the eye of an angel:

1. The Almighty nudged nothingness and anti-nothingness causing them to collide and set off a chain of events know as Doublelarity or The Big Bang.

2. The Almighty caused the Angel Methuselah to visit Earth and establish the fact that people of different metabolism could have different life spans.

3. The Almighty caused the Angel Noah to use his different metabolism to live a long life and survive the flood.

4. The Teacher is also depicted as having a 'halo', presumably given by The Almighty to facilitate his changing wavelengths and moving from one dimension to another.

5. Abraham and his 'Angelic powers' is a common ancestor in many religions.

6. The Angel Moses was another 'long-life' and could have conferred with other Angels for forty days and forty nights prior to writing the Ten Commandments.

7. The Angel Buddha was another spiritual leader who often referred to abandoning his earthly body in favor of eternal life.

8. The Angel Confucius was supposedly born into poverty yet wrote many rules for behavior and ethics – a thinking

and contemplation level far above his earthbound contemporaries.

9. After conferring with an Angel, Mohammed instructed his followers to stop worshipping idols – he also frequently communicated with God through (other) Angels.

CHAPTER 6
The Annihilation in 2012

December 21, 2012 is a very ill omened year when total annihilation is, in deed, a possibility. Science is not taking that date very seriously so it is up to us individually to prepare for any eventuality that may present itself on that date. The need for wavelength management is real and the December date will be its first test and probably mean the difference between whether we live in another dimension or die in this dimension. Our Government has failed to emphasize wavelength research/importance so we are vulnerable for whatever cosmic forces present themselves in 2012. Nor has the Government given us any instructions to follow should doom come from outer space. For instance, on December Twenty-first in the year Two Thousand Twelve, are we supposed to head for high ground, or move underground, or head inland, or get in a hot air balloon, or migrate toward the equator or move toward the poles? On that date, The Earth will be in the middle of many unusual forces, some from our own geomagnetic field, some from galactic alignment, and some from our nearest star, the sun. Here is a case where wavelength management will allow us to escape into another world to assure our survival. The Earth is in the midst of a magnetic pole change, a sort of summersault between the North magnetic pole and the South magnetic pole. It has happened before and, yes it is a very slow process but we are going through that process right now. Another factor is the galactic alignments on December 21, 2012. That is when Saturn and Jupiter are aligned with the Sun. In the past, such alignment has been strong enough to make our Sun wobble, especially during its eleven-year cycle when its magnetic field reverses. And, on a larger scale, there is some hocus-pocus about our solar system traversing the plane of the Milky Way on that same day, 12.21.2012. Complicated? Yes, so let us illustrate. Let us compare the Milky Way with Saturn where many bits and pieces orbit in a relatively narrow ring around the planet. The solar systems in the Milky Way also form a narrow ring as they revolve around their galactic center and on December 21st of the aforementioned year, the Milky Way will be in the center of that ring perfectly aligned between our sun and whatever black hole is in the center of our galaxy. Probably hocus-pocus but if Saturn and Jupiter have an effect on our Sun, will some unusual alignment within the Milky Way have a similar gravitational effect and make it wobble once again? Let us go to the third unusual event scheduled to occur on December 21, 2012 and that is when our Sun flips its polarity and returns to its eleven-year cycle of increased solar flare activity. During previous periods of increased solar activity, we experienced cell phone disruptions, power outages and radio blackouts. Combine a flip in polarity with a wobble and who knows what chaos will ensue.

Since the total combination of cosmic anomalies has not happened in recorded history, how do we determine their combined cause and effect? They all focus on December 21, 2012 and that day has been know for centuries to be the winter solstice, the day that our Sun is at its greatest distance opposite the polar hemisphere, the day when we would be most vulnerable should all those other celestial forces combine and present themselves. Will the cosmic energy on that day cause the Earth to resonate and become unstable, just as Jupiter and Saturn make the Sun wobble, or will those forces, if any, accelerate the geomagnetic flip of our poles? What happens if we resonate at the same time we are being bombarded by solar storms? Will there be worldwide tsunamis, increased earthquake and volcanic activity or will a summersault in the Earth's magnetic field raise havoc with airline guidance systems? Yes, December 21, 2012 is a very ominous date so let us focus on wavelength management and either skip into our tomorrows to see whatever the impact will be, or seek refuge in another universe. The Russians are ready for December 21st as they have what is known as Yamantau Mountain, a huge underground complex in the Ural Mountains. Originally designed to survive nuclear warfare, the mountain complex is conveniently available to protect as many as 60,000 people should our Earth start to wobble and generate catastrophes. Cheyenne Mountain may house a few of our dignitaries but what about the rest of us should our magnetosphere crumble and allow the deadly solar borealis to blast through our atmosphere and scorch the Earth? The bunkers near Washington DC were designed to protect the politicians – seems strange that they would save themselves, especially if there were going to be no citizens left to govern. We have saved the dignitaries, we have saved the politicians, but what are we doing to save the parents of future generations? Eighteen thousand years ago the Earth wobbled, tilted just one degree and brought on the beginning of a new ice age. If that wobble and one-degree tilt resulted in an ice age, what will the 2012 wobble bring?

Scientists are always dramatic when they talk about earthquakes and other natural phenomena. Their favorite phrase is 'It's not a matter of IF it is going to happen, it's a matter of WHEN it is going to happen' and in the process, the need for preparation takes a back seat to phraseology. Yes, California will have a big earthquake but will the big one come in ten years, a hundred years or will it be in ten hundred years – the time frame is irrelevant as long as we are preparing for it. Part of any reasonable preparation is to re-discover how Edgar Cayce manipulated his 'sleep' waves long enough to peek into the future. Wavelength research and management is our key to survival – let us be dramatic right back at the scientists and say "Wavelength research and management or annihilation, the choice is yours".

Let us promote wavelength management and hopefully we will be able to peek into our tomorrows for some reassurance that there will be no 2012 catastrophe, or zoom into another dimension to escape calamity and continue our existence in His image.

CHAPTER 7
Wavelength Management

As previously mentioned there will be a growing need for wavelength management, both for ensuring our survival in 2012 or maybe some other future calamity, and also for recreation amongst other things. Vacuum tubes evolved into transistors, and transistors evolved into microchips, and now we have computers everywhere – are we just a discovery or two away from wavelength management and inter-universe travel? Wavelength management does not mean someone else controlling your brainwaves but it means researching techniques and methods for you to control and manage your own waves. Unfortunately, the scientific discipline of wavelength management does not yet exist so we need to develop an interest in the area and recruit experts from such fields as quantum mechanics, string theory, theoretical physics, physiology plus visionaries from related studies. Science lines up well with historical events and famous names from olden times but it fails miserably when lining up with the needs of the future. A recent proposed government budget included monies for pig odor research, grape research and blueberry research, but nil, zero, zilch for the preservation of mankind. Plus we have somewhat of a warped sense of financial responsibility, i.e., we pay athletes far more than we pay people to teach our children the academics and other tools needed for the difficult years ahead. In that line we need to encourage our leaders to be proactive about our tomorrows rather than wait and be reactive to what our tomorrows may bring. If leaders can not get interested in academics and saving our tomorrows, maybe they will continue their high interest in sports and allocate funds for virtual reality where wavelength managers could insert you into a super bowl game, or set you up for an out of this world affair with your favorite staffer or maybe your neighbor – would not the politicians love that one – mental or wavelength adultery and not subject to voter repercussion. Joking and quipping aside, here is what wavelength management could do for us, especially when delving into the past:

Judicial research – maybe the supreme court justices could slide into the fourth dimension and zip back into the revolutionary era and get first hand knowledge of what our founders were thinking when they wrote the very ambiguous Second Amendment. Or the Justices could get first hand knowledge of what our founders meant by the word 'compelled' in the Fifth Amendment – did they really intend to forbid the truth from being told or did they mean to forbid 'compelled' self-incrimination (check any thesaurus - compel and coerce are interchangeable). Then what were our Founders thinking when they wrote of lifetime appointments to the Supreme Court? In the 1700s the term lifetime appointment meant ten or twelve years as the courts' checks and balances were governed by limited life expectancy, which was only thirty to forty years at that time. Like linguistics change so does life expectancy and, by today's standards, life expectancy has more than doubled which means a Justice could serve as many as three decades on the bench and, most frightenly, serve without any checks and balances. As a matter of fact, in early America it was questionable that the 'average' pilgrim could live for three decades let alone serve three decades on the bench. Another area where time traveling justices could investigate is that of separation of church and state. Again, once we place our justices in the 1700s they will realize that King George III was the motivator for our First Amendment. Yes, at that time, King George III wore two hats – one hat was King of England and the other hat was Head of the Church of England. Yes, the King controlled both the political sector and the religious sector at the same time; and since his influence was so intertwined, a tithe could very well end up in the tax collector's coffer or even the Crown's pocket. As result of commingling funds, our Founders very eloquently wrote the First Amendment. It was great back in the 1700s when our framers eliminated the state/church coffer connection but, at the same time, they kept 'In God We Trust' and all the other mottos that sustain and emphasize our religious beliefs. Oops, etymology steps in and over time the memory of King George III putting tithes in his own pocket lost its significance and the amendment has since been re-defined to eliminate those mottos and religious traditions that have long been an integral part of our precious culture. That brings us to Cruel and Unusual Punishment. A quick trip back to the 1700s will show that during the pre-revolutionary years, many crimes carried capital punishment, including horse stealing, adultery and in Virginia, even stealing grapes was a capital crime. As result our Founders coined the term 'cruel and unusual punishment' to help make punishment fit the crime. Execution was obviously cruel and unusual for someone stealing grapes and such extreme punishment was quickly reduced as it was with many other crimes. On our Justices' trip back into history, they will quickly notice that our Founders were tough on adultery and then realize that over the years the Supreme Court had re-defined our framers intent and allowed the pendulum swing too far in the opposite direction. How could the Court do that? Oh yes, its separation of church and state again – no more Ten Commandments to be the Court's conscience.

Crack crimes – we already mentioned solving the 1994 Brentwood murder (it is not the ballplayer after all) but what about some other crimes. Neither Jack The Ripper nor The Boston Strangler was convicted of their horrific crimes. Marilyn Monroe's demise also drew unusual speculations and a trip back into history would easily rule in/rule out any political connection and explain why there was no overdose residue in her intestinal tract. And Jimmy Hoffa, what ever happened to him anyway? Was his disappearance mob revenge or was it another kind of assassination? Speaking about assassination, a quick trip back to the grassy knoll would confirm whatever notoriety the knoll may or may not have. Then, do we dare mention the horrific and ask investigators to step into history and solve the JonBenet case? And, what about the disappearance in Aruba? Although we would not be able to preclude the events from happening, rewinding history may solve these cases relatively quickly. Perhaps some day, after wavelength research and management becomes an accepted principle, we can put a quarter into the time machine, follow the 'change wavelength' instructions and zip back to those famous crime scenes and solve those cases that have puzzled us for years.

The future of wavelength management can actually start with you. Edgar Cayce dozed off and zipped into the future, so the next time you are about to zonk off, pause a moment and try to grab a passing wave. It is trial and error so do not give up. Success usually comes after numerous failures so be persistent and be the first to re-discover the path into our tomorrows.